It was springtime, and the park sparrows were
chirping merrily in the hedgerow.
Haris kicked the ball, wet with dew,
to his cousin Sienna, who shrieked
with laughter as she raced towards it.
"You beat me again!" he smiled,
shaking his head.

1

Haris flung himself across the grass,
making Sienna laugh even more.
The children chased the ball further across the park.
It rolled near to the park gardener,
who had stopped cutting the grass
to look at something on the ground.

"What is it?" asked Haris, peering down.
"It's a hedgehog," replied the man slowly.
"But I think I may have hurt him accidentally
with the grass cutter.
"Hetch-hog hurt," said Sienna.

3

Haris thought for a moment.
"Our grandad is a vet and lives next door to me," he said.
"My house is just over there – that one,
with the green door. I can take him there."
He pointed to show the gardener where he meant.
"You'll need my gloves to carry him." said the man,
"Hedgehogs are prickly, be very gentle."

Haris carried the hedgehog to his house
as carefully as he could,
cradled in the gardener's thick gloves.
His mum stood in the doorway,
she'd been watching the children playing.
"What have you got there, Haris?" she asked.
"Hetch-hog!" said Sienna. "It's not well, it's hurt."

"I'm going to take it to Grandad," said Haris.
"The gardener hit him with the mower but it was an accident.
He's really hurt mum, he needs help."
"OK then," she said.
"But dinner is nearly ready so don't be long.
If your grandad is busy then just leave
the poor little thing with him, he will know what to do."

Haris let Sienna race ahead to ring the bell
as he carried the injured hedgehog steadily.
The door opened and there stood
Professor Newman, wearing his white vet's coat.
"What have we here?" he asked, kindly.
"It's a hedgehog Grandad," said Haris.
"He's badly hurt. Can you help?"

7

"Hetch-hog has a poorly leg and sore eye."
said Sienna, scrunching her own eyes up to show
what she meant. Professor Newman nodded.
"Bring it through to the medical room," he said.
"No time to waste. You were right to bring him to me."

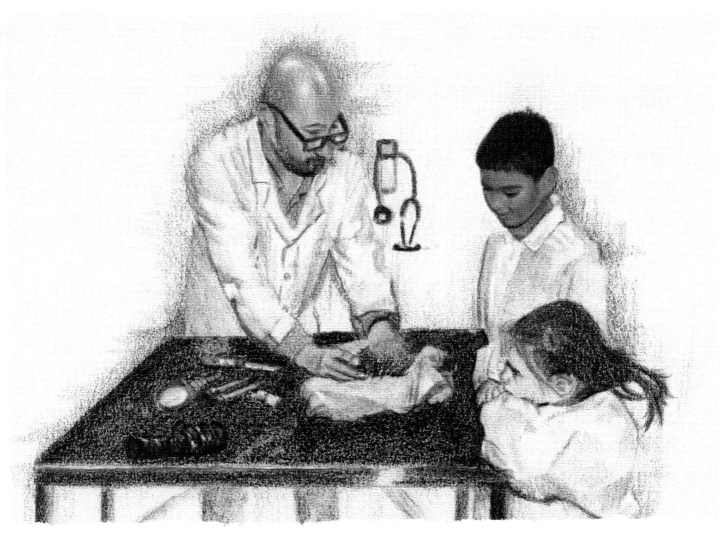

The children watched anxiously as their grandfather
carefully unwrapped the glove from the injured hedgehog.
"He's in a bad way alright," he told them.
"But I might have just the thing! Did you know
I'm not just a vet? I also make
models and robots and I think this hedgehog
could be my first real test subject!"

Professor Newman went to his desk and fetched
four metal rods, a few wires, also some microchips
and laid them all out by the motionless hedgehog.
"I'll need to work quickly," he said.
"Could you pass me my special glasses ?"
He then added some thick microscopic lenses
to his glasses to help him see clearer.

Next, he put a tiny mask over the hedgehog's face
and attached it to a pump which puffed air
to help the hedgehog breathe while he worked.
"Will Hetch be OK?" asked Sienna in a small voice.
"I'll do my best," her grandfather assured her.
Haris crossed his fingers hard.

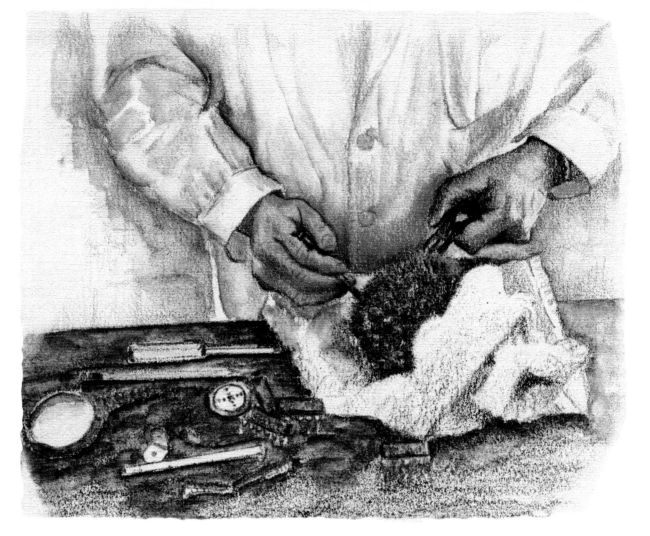

"The hedgehog's eye and back legs are badly damaged,
so I will replace them with mechanical ones," their grandfather told them.
"You two need to go and have your dinner while I do the operation."
"Can we come back after?" the children begged.
"Yes you can come back as long as you help
wash the dishes from your dinner," he laughed.

The operation was soon over and the children were knocking
at the door again. Their grandfather led them through to the medical room
once more. The hedgehog lay very still. Haris and Sienna stood silently
not knowing what to say. "I need you two to look after him for a moment,"
said their grandfather. "I just need to make a quick phone call."

Haris crept to the door. He knew it was wrong to listen
but he was so worried about the hedgehog.
He needed to know what was happening.
"I tried a new operation," he heard his grandfather say.
"Yes, a hedgehog.
But he's very poorly – I'm not sure he's going to make it."

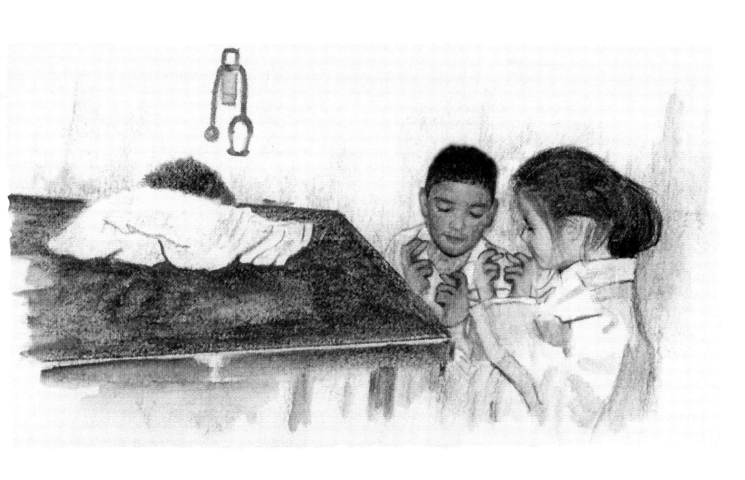

Haris ran back to Sienna. "We need to do something,"
he said. "Hetch is really ill."
"I know how we can help Hetch," said Sienna firmly.
"We need wishes." Sienna then closed her eyes
and crossed her fingers. "Wish Hetch get better,"
she whispered. Haris copied Sienna
and they wished, as hard as they could.

And as they wished, a single tear trickled down
Sienna's cheek, ran down her chin,
and dripped with a tiny "plop"
– right into the lifeless hedgehog's new robotic eye.
For a moment there was silence. And then....
Fizz! Flash, a spark shot out!

The eye flashed red! Then blue!
And then red again!
The hedgehog's other eye opened and
he gave a deep sigh, a big yawn, and a biiiiig stretch.
And then, without any warning whatsoever,
something so amazing happened that
Haris and Sienna couldn't believe it was real.
The hedgehog spoke!

17

"Hello," it said. "Where am I?"
The children stared at it in amazement.
"Grandad!" yelled Haris. "You have GOT to come and see this!"

Professor Newman raced into the room. "What happened?"
"We made a wish for him to get better and he did" said Haris excitedly.
"Hetch talk, Hetch talk, his name Hetch" shouted Sienna,
clapping her hands together in delight.
"Who are you?" asked the hedgehog
"I'm Haris, this is Sienna
and this is our grandad, Professor Newman, he made you better!"

"Was I hurt?" asked the hedgehog.
"Yes," said Haris. "You were badly injured.
our grandad has given you new legs, and a new eye,
just like a real life robot! Would you like to see?"
The hedgehog looked scared.
"OK" he said, after a pause. "I'm ready."

Haris fetched a small mirror and the hedgehog saw his strange new appearance.
"We had to rebuild you," said Professor Newman, gently. "You're going to be OK."
The hedgehog was quiet for a moment.
"Thank you," he whispered. "It's a lot to take in."

"I've treated a lot of hedgehogs in my time," said the clever Vet.
But you're the first I've ever been able to fix like this!"
The hedgehog inspected his new metal legs,
and swivelled his robotic eye.
"It will take a bit of getting used to," he said eventually.
"But I'm so glad you helped me. What can I do to say thank you?"

Then Professor Newman had an idea,
"Would you like to help other Wildlife that's in trouble?
It gives you a great feeling to know you're doing your bit."
Hetch wasn't sure what "doing your bit" meant, but it sounded good.

"What can I do to help?" he asked.
"With your new microchip, you can gather and store all kinds
of information about wildlife, just like a computer!
You see, there aren't as many birds, bees, flowers, frogs,
or hedgehogs anymore. And we need everyone to help."
"YOU'LL BE A SUPER HERO FOR NATURE !" exclaimed Haris.

"How can people help nature?" asked Hetch, confused.
"By building ponds, planting flowers and trees,
and letting a bit of their garden go wild,"
said Professor Newman. "And that's just the start!"
Hetch looked thoughtful. "I will be glad to help," he said.
"But would you mind terribly if I waited until tomorrow? I'm a bit tired right now
and my tummy is ever so empty!" Everyone laughed. Hetch smiled back.

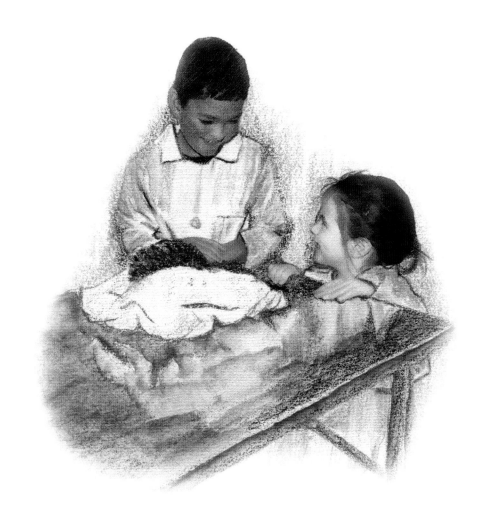

"Of course," said the professor. "We'll get you something to eat now."
"And you can stay with me!" said Haris excitedly.
"With your new legs and eye I'm going to call you Robo Hog!"
"No his name is HETCH, silly." Sienna told Haris.

Hetch gobbled up an enormous dinner of cat food. Soon after Sienna's daddy collected her. Haris then took Hetch home for a rest. "We will need an early night." said Haris. "You've been through a lot." The little hedgehog lay down in a small bed that Haris had made for him. Hetch thought about everything that had happened that day. He knew it would take time to adjust, but he was also very excited about what lay ahead. Tomorrow was going to be the start of a whole new set of adventures.

As he drifted off to sleep all the events of the day
appeared in his dreams.
A little tune came into his head and the words soon followed.
This is the song he dreamt of that night...

"When nature's in trouble, and the birds have flown away,
The bees are disappearing, who can save the day?
Open up your garden & feed the birds,
And you will hear them singing their song.
Plant lots of trees and flowers, and leave your grass long.

Build a pond for the frogs and toads,
& make a waterfall for the creatures to bathe.
WE NEED TO DO IT NOW.
Robo hog, Robo hog.

A small hole in the fence or a gate will allow us hedgehogs in to wander.
A pile of leaves or a pile of logs can be our home and just leave out a dish of water.
Robo hog – The superhero for nature.
And I'm here to gather all the data.
So you know it all.
Robo hog, Robo hog.

It's true what they say, it's true what they say,
If you build it they will come.
It's true what they say, it's true what they say,
If you build it we will come

I'm Robo hog – The superhero for nature.
And I'm here to gather all the data.
Robo hog, Robo hog.
So you know it all."

If you would like to hear the song he dreamt that night just scan the QR code on Hetch's tummy.

Top tips to help Hedgehogs in your garden.

1. A shallow bowl of water.
2. High protein dog/cat biscuits.
3. Their natural food - bugs & beetles,
might like a pile of logs, leaves or a bug hotel.
4. If you don't have a shed or decking they can
 get under then, build a hedgehog house to sleep,
have baby hoglets or to hibernate in.
5. A 4"x4" hole in your fence or gate to allow
them into wander.
6. If you see one out in the daytime then check your
local rescue for advice.

David Doughty

Passionate wildlife photographer - has been up close with Wolves, Lions, Lemurs, Puffins, Otters and many other creatures.
On his first day working for a conservation charity David couldn't believe the amount of endangered species in the UK.
He knew he couldn't help them all and so decided to put much of his spare time into helping one creature. But what would it be ...
David had built a robotic hedgehog for his charity stall to catch peoples attention, his boss called it Robo Hog and a seed was planted for a series of books.
And he knew what animal he would try to save.

Gary Theobald

Suffolk based, award winning, coloured pencil artist.
Has featured in numerous publications, including International Artist magazine, in 2007. Artwork held in private collections in the UK and Europe.

Special thanks to Haris & Sienna
for acting out the scenes.

Cheers Gary - here's to our first book,
you have been very patient with me.

Thanks also to Alison Folwell for your invaluable help
with proof reading, advice and editing of the text.

Dedicated to all my Grandchildren
and
to all those that help our wildlife.

David Doughty